# The Red Geranium

## Janette Oke

**BETHANY HOUSE PUBLISHERS**
MINNEAPOLIS, MINNESOTA 55438

Cover illustration by Jennifer Heyd Wharton.
Book insides designed by Sherry Paavola.

Copyright © 1995
Janette Oke

Published by Bethany House Publishers
A Ministry of Bethany Fellowship, Inc.
11300 Hampshire Avenue South
Minneapolis, Minnesota 55438

Printed in the United States of America.

ISBN 1-55661-662-7

*To our forebears
who have given so much of themselves
to make our lives richer.*

# BOOKS BY JANETTE OKE

*Janette Oke's Reflections on the Christmas Story*

## SEASONS OF THE HEART

## LOVES COMES SOFTLY

## CANADIAN WEST

## WOMEN OF THE WEST

## DEVOTIONALS

*Janette Oke: Heart for the Prairie*
Biography of Janette Oke by Laurel Oke Logan

*The Oke Family Cookbook*
by Barbara Oke and Deborah Oke

JANETTE OKE was born in Champion, Alberta, during the depression years, to a Canadian prairie farmer and his wife. She is a graduate of Mountain View Bible College in Didsbury, Alberta, where she met her husband, Edward. They were married in May of 1957, and went on to pastor churches in Indiana as well as Calgary and Edmonton, Canada.

The Okes have three sons and one daughter and are enjoying the addition of grandchildren to the family. Edward and Janette have both been active in their local church, serving various capacities as Sunday school teachers and board members. They make their home near Calgary, Alberta.

**S**he moved restlessly as she mentally groped toward full consciousness after another night of troubled sleep. She disliked the feeling of her hair in her face. She was used to it being neatly tucked into the gray braid that she carefully pinned at the nape of her neck during the day and released each evening to hang loosely down her back. She tried to push the wayward hair back—to free her face from the silvery strands. Her hand didn't obey her. And then she remembered —

She was no longer at home in her familiar bedroom with the soft, rose-patterned wallpaper and the lacy window curtains. She was not in her high-posted brass bed with the quilt she had made with her own hands spread out over her. No wonder she felt so strange, so unattached.

Her eyes opened wide as though the memory startled her. But she had already dealt with the personal loss.

Or at least she thought she had.

She stared at the stark whiteness of the four walls around her. "Whipped cream" they called the color, rather than just plain old white. But it reminded her very little of the warm and fluffy cream that she had lavishly ladled onto her freshly baked cream pies.

Her eyes went to the large, bare window with its beige venetian blind closed against the light. "So handy," they had said. "You can let in just as much light as you decide you want."

She hated the ugly blind. She wanted all the light. All the light. And she wanted softness. Softness, a few frills. The cold, stark window didn't draw her—not to finger a soft curtain as it was drawn back and slipped into the ties at the side. She could not look out on dew-damp lawn and carefully trimmed beds of daisies and forget-me-nots as she welcomed a new day. There was nothing but a concrete street beyond this window. A concrete street filled with impatient cars. She knew that. With effort she turned her back to it—and once again she cried. Soft, quiet tears that squeezed from under her eyelids and trickled slowly down the seams of her weathered face.

An hour later they came for her. Two of them in baby-blue uniforms and purposely cheerful morning greetings. They smiled—professional smiles, she called them. She wondered how many times during the night they had been called. How many troubled sleepers had they tried to calm? Well, their shift would soon be over and they would be off to their own homes again. Homes where waking children and piles of laundry awaited them. She didn't envy them their double load—and yet—

"How are we this morning, Mrs. Thomas?" She couldn't speak for them, but they didn't wait for her mumbled answer anyway. "It's another nice day. Let's get you up and ready for breakfast. What do you wish to wear today? Something pretty—and comfy. It's therapy day again."

One went to give the venetian blind a quick twist to show her what a lovely day it was, the other proceeded to open her wardrobe so she could choose a dress for the day. Her eyes fell on her familiar housedresses, then drifted to the new ones her daughters had bought for her when she was to be admitted—just like she was going on some exciting vacation trip. She hadn't yet learned to like the new dresses. They didn't seem to fit into her life any more than the plain room and the stiff venetian blinds.

"That blue one," she managed with little enthusiasm. She was thankful that the nurse understood her. Her speech was gradually getting a bit better. For one fleeting moment she dared to hope that she would get well—that she would be able to return home again. Back to—but, no. Her home wasn't hers any longer. The small house was to be sold. The belongings—all the things she had used in daily chores, the things she had fashioned to make the house a home, the things that had come to be her treasures—all would be scattered here and there. Like leaves on the autumn wind, once gone, she knew even in her confusion, they would never be able to be collected, gathered, put back again into proper place. The small house would never be her home again.

*H*e sat on his front steps, one hand idly toying with the collar of Mutt, the lop-eared dog who was his best friend, the other hand lying still in his lap, moist from clinging to the nickel Gran Thomas had given him. He was not surprised that she had remembered. His great-grand-mother always gave him a nickel whenever he went to see her. But under the present circumstance the customary small gift had brought a strange look to his mother's face and she had turned quickly, like she did when she didn't want him to see her tears.

He couldn't understand about Gran Thomas. Oh, he knew all about her being sick. His folks had carefully explained why she needed to leave her little house and move in "where she could be properly cared for." He couldn't figure out everything about old age and strokes and stuff. But he did know that it all had changed a lot of things. There no longer were the stops at Gran's house, the house that smelled of fresh-baked ginger cookies and tangy apple pies. There no longer was the gentle swaying of the back porch swing as they sat and rocked together, the squeak of the wicker chair on the front porch as she sat with her needlework and watched him play. There were no trips to her little garden to pull crisp carrots that could be rinsed under the outside tap and eaten on the spot.

He missed it. Missed Gran Thomas. It wasn't the same to go and see her in her "new home." Not the same at all. Her room was strange, even though it held a scattering of the familiar—like the mantel clock up on her shelf. He knew that his great-grandfather Thomas had given the clock to her as an engagement gift. She treasured it, that clock, and one of her daily tasks had been to take the key from the secret drawer in the big roll-top oak desk and wind the timepiece carefully each morning.

It was silent now—no comfortable ticking to mark the passing minutes. Silent and still. The hands were eternally at nine minutes past one. It wasn't right. Someone should fix the clock. He had spoken to his mother about it. "Oh, it's not broken," she had responded lightly. "It just needs winding."

"Then wind it," he had protested, which had earned a stern look. "I—I mean," he stammered, not quite ready to apologize for his outburst, "can't you wind it? Please."

"I don't come in often enough," replied his mother. "It needs to be wound every day. It would just stop again."

"Why don't the nurses—?"

"The nurses have more than enough to do without winding clocks," responded his mother with a sigh that said she was about as tired as the overworked nurses.

But it troubled him. The silent clock. The bare walls that "couldn't have nail holes." The floors polished and devoid of all rugs that "could be tripped on." He didn't like Gran Thomas' new home. It didn't suit her. It looked different. It smelled different. It was no wonder that Gran wasn't getting better.

His hand moved from the dog collar and his fingers entangled themselves in Mutt's curly fur. He opened his other sweaty hand and stared at the coin he held in the palm. Tears formed in the deep blue eyes.

"We gotta do something, Mutt," he

whispered to his dog. "We gotta help her."

Help her? How could the two of them help her? His folks had explained that she had nurses for her care and therapy people who worked to strengthen lost muscles and nutritionists who coaxed her to eat and doctors who gave her medicines.

But was any of it really working? He wondered.

He knew that something was all wrong. The whole thing felt wrong. It wasn't just the room. It was Gran

Thomas. She looked so sad—like she really couldn't be happy, like she had nothing to live for anymore. Oh, her eyes lit up when he came, and she managed one of her lopsided smiles. But he knew—he just knew—that something was missing. A lot was missing. All of her sparkle and fun and secret-sharing was gone. It was like—like some kind of light inside had gone out. And he didn't know what to do about it.

The morning passed. She managed to get past breakfast, though it bothered her a lot to be dripping porridge on her hospital bib like an infant experimenting with a spoon. She who had always been so careful about personal grooming now could do little to tend to herself.

And then it was off to therapy. She didn't like therapy. Besides the pain, there was the reminder of just how much she had lost to the stroke. She always was glad when the session was over and she was returned to the silence of her own room, bleak as it was.

Family members would come in the afternoon. Someone always did. She wondered absently if they had a schedule all worked out. Tuesday is Mary's turn. Wednesday, Sarah's—and on and on. She loved them—her family. She did wish she wasn't the cause for this added burden to their already full schedules. They were all so busy—had so much to tend to. And now this. She shook her head slowly, sadness darkening her eyes. She couldn't bear it without their calls. She wondered if she was being selfish. But she needed them. Needed them just to get through another day.

Her eyes traveled to the top of the dresser and over the worn Bible that lay there. It was the only item on the smooth surface. Staff did not have time to "lift and shuffle clutter when dusting," she'd been informed. Most personal items had to be tucked into

drawers. But she had insisted that the
Bible be left out. She could no longer
hold it and turn its pages with her
clumsy hands—but at least she could
have the small comfort of seeing it
there. And it was a comfort. And yet—
yet even her desire to gather joy and
hope and peace from its daily reading
had forsaken her. Where was that
inner flame, that solid underpinning to
her life that her faith had given her?

Suddenly she felt very old—and
very tired.

*H*e had thought, had hoped and prayed, that it would soon end—that Gran would quickly get better and return to her own home. He felt a sick sensation inside when his mother came out their front door to announce another visit to the hospital room.

"Isn't Gran better yet?" he asked, looking up at her from his position on the steps.

"Better? Oh my, no," said his mother. "She has been very sick and—"

But he quickly cut in, "How much longer?"

His mother's eyes grew wet and her chin trembled. "I don't know," she murmured, shaking her head. "None of us know."

"But—but how long until she can come home?" he persisted.

She reached for him then. Reached for him and held him up against her dress with the pretty pink and blue flowers. Her hand stroked his unruly mop of tawny hair.

"She won't be able to come home again, ever—even—even when she gets better. She—she'll need care—"

He pushed away from her to look up into her face, his eyes large with the horror of what she had just said. "Never?" His voice sounded strange. Squeaky.

She didn't answer with words. She just shook her head. Her chin was trembling again.

"Who—who'll take care of her flowers? Her house?" he managed, remembering the love Gran had lavished on her little home—her potted plants and tidy flower beds, the vegetable garden in back.

"We'll—we'll find someone to—to take her flowers. We'll give them away. Neighbors or—I'm sure that someone will—" His mother stopped and didn't say anything for a while. Then she pulled him closer. "Her house is being sold, Tommy," she explained gently but firmly, and from her tone he knew she wanted him to listen carefully. To listen and understand.

The very words seemed to tear him from the world he had known. He couldn't comprehend them—couldn't even bear to think about them. He pulled from his mother's arms and ran out the kitchen door. He had to know if it was true.

Mutt joined him as he hurried from the yard. They ran the few blocks to his great-grandmother's little home, and all the way he was hoping that his mother was wrong.

As he rounded the corner he saw the unfamiliar sign. He sounded out

the words—F-O-R S-A-L-E. It was true.
The little house was going to be sold.
There it was—with the trim patch of
green lawn, the beds of blooming
forget-me-nots and shasta daisies. He
shifted his attention to the house and
let his eyes move upward. Up to the
window. The window where Gran
always seemed to be standing—watch-
ing for him. She wasn't there now.
The curtain hung limply, not aside as
it always was when he came. He
could scarcely see the red of the gera-
niums that sat blooming on the sill.

He turned away, an empty feeling inside, and started walking slowly toward home. Mutt seemed to sense his mood and nearly tripped him, pressing up against him as a whine formed in the dog's throat.

Tommy's heavy steps were moving him away when the thought hit him. He had to do something. He just had to. He turned back to the little house, his heart pounding. He wasn't sure that what he was about to do was the right thing—and Gran always reminded him over and over to always, *always* do the right thing. But everything else that was happening was the wrong thing. How could he ever sort it out?

S he sat quietly in the rocker, limp hands folded in her lap. She was glad for the rocker. It was one comforting bit of home that she had been able to bring with her.

But she didn't actually rock. She had no interest in rocking. She had just finished another visit with the therapist. "You must try harder," the woman had said. "If you want to use your hand again, you must try harder."

It wasn't that she hadn't taken on difficult challenges in her lifetime. There had been many tough things to face over her years. She had always met them head on before. Had always fought her way through. But now— now there seemed no good reason to put in all the effort. What could she gain? What would be the purpose? She stared dully at the corner cupboard where the blank TV screen reflected her somber face. Everything she loved was already lost to her. Why should she work hard to hang on to—nothing?

*H*e couldn't reach the latch on the back gate, so he had to squeeze through the spot in the fence where one board could be coaxed to the side. He had discovered the secret long ago and hadn't told Gran about it. She would have had the board fixed and that would have spoiled it for him. He thought of it as his private passage and sneaked in and out through the opening when no one was looking. Mutt always slid through the hole with him. Tommy thought that Mutt enjoyed the little game almost as much as he did himself.

He pushed through the narrow opening and stood waiting for his little dog. His hand reached to the small dog's collar, urging him in a silent message to be quiet as they made their approach to the beloved little house.

Cautiously he moved up the back walk, his heart thumping wildly in his small chest.

"I hope it's still there," he whispered

to Mutt.

The dog looked up at him and then gave one quick lick at the hand that had dropped back to the boy's side.

It took a bit of squirming to work his way in between the bushes in the back corner by the porch. The up-turned pot was still there. Had anyone disturbed it? With all his heart he hoped not.

He held his breath as he carefully turned it over. Yes, the small tin box. Now if only—

It was hard to open the box with the tight-fitting cover. After some struggling, his tongue working hard against the corner of his mouth, he at last managed to pry the lid from the small container. One heart-stopping moment, and there it was. Safe. The secret key to Gran's back door.

He was glad she had let him hide it there. Only the two of them knew about it. "You will never be locked out of my house—not day or night," she had told him. "If you ever need me, you just get that key and come on in."

It had been their little secret. Their little promise to one another. He had felt very important and special as they planned the hiding place and she had watched him tuck it away.

Now he clasped the key tightly and moved stealthily toward the back door. His glance traveled from side to side. Was it okay to use the key now? Now that the house was for sale? He wasn't sure—but he knew—he knew he *had* to do something. He couldn't just let Gran— But he didn't finish the thought.

"What's in the bag?" His mother looked at him quizzically as he clambered past her and in through the big side door of the van. He had been hoping she wouldn't notice.

He had to answer—and his answer had to be truthful.

"It's for Gran," he replied, his eyes lowering.

He was sure she would press him

further, but to his surprise she let it pass.

"Get in then," she prompted him. "We don't have much time."

He scampered quickly into the seat and buckled up. He wished to avoid any further attention.

When they reached the hospital, his heart was pounding. He had hated these trips to Gran's "new home," but today he felt differently about it. He was anxious to get there and to see Gran. He somehow felt that the bag he carried could help to put some

things to right. Now if only—if only
his plan worked. If only his mother
wouldn't say, "You can't bring that in,"
or the nurses wouldn't ask, "What do
you think you're doing?" If only—

He felt small and scared. He
wished he had Mutt with him.

But his mother hurried him along
the wide concrete walk toward the big
heavy doors. She didn't seem to even
notice that he was still carrying the
paper bag. Her thoughts could have
been miles away. She looked like she
was biting her lip.

He cast nervous glances at the
nurses as they hurried down the long,
blank halls. Not one seemed to even
glance his way. He walked quickly
beside his mother, hoping that her
swishing skirts would help to hide his
package.

"Hello, Grandma," his mother said
in her cheerful voice as soon as they
entered the antiseptic-smelling room,
and she put on a brave smile.

She bent to kiss the elderly woman
on the cheek.

"How are you today?" she asked

Janette Oke

affectionately, patting the paper-thin
skin of the listless hand on the arm of
the rocking chair.

"Good—all considered," Gran managed through uncooperative lips. That
had been her pat answer for many
years. It was truthful—and Gran insisted on truth—and yet it gave nothing
away. She did not wish to further
burden her beloved family with her
own despair.

She looked around as though
seeking something and then her eyes
fell on Tommy. They immediately

brightened.

"You came," she murmured, reaching her good hand toward him.

He moved forward then, his bulky paper bag a hindrance to the hug he attempted to give her.

"Hi, Gran," he said, his voice hushed. He felt a need for secrecy. She looked puzzled.

"You got a cold?" she asked him, concern edging her voice.

He shook his head.

She still frowned slightly.

"I brought you something." He

continued to whisper.

He didn't know what to say or do with his package. He wasn't sure if his mother should be allowed to see. But he didn't know how to get the contents to Gran without his mother knowing. He stepped back and stood awkwardly, shifting the bag back and forth.

"What is it?" asked Gran, but her voice didn't have the same enthusiasm she had always had for their secrets in the past.

He looked up at his mother again,

uncertainty making his mouth twitch.

"Well, go ahead and show her," his mother prompted. Then to the elderly woman she hurried on, "I've no idea what he has brought. It was all his idea—his doing. I don't even know where he got whatever it is." She laughed a little nervously. "I suppose he's sharing one of his special 'treasures.' Tommy really misses you, Grandma. We all do."

He still fidgeted.

"Well, all right," his mother continued. "Show Gran what you've brought for her. Go ahead."

He managed to get his legs and arms to move. He pressed up against Gran's bony knees and put the brown paper bag on her robe-covered lap. Carefully he unwound the scrunched-down paper. As the last crumpled edge was straightened the elderly woman peeped into the bag. Tommy moved so he could look into it with her. Together their eyes fell on the contents at the same time.

He expected her to make some comment, but she said nothing.

Quickly he looked up. Was she disappointed? But no—he saw the light in her face and he knew—knew that she liked his gift.

Then tears were running down her crinkled cheeks and dripping softly onto the brown of the paper. One trembling hand reached into the bag and awkwardly lifted the contents out onto her lap.

"Oh, it's got a broken leaf," he said in alarm, reaching out a hand to try to repair what the trip in the bag had done.

But his great-grandmother seemed not to notice. Lovingly her hand caressed one smooth leaf after another.

"Where'd you get that?" he heard his mother ask, but her voice was soft, tender.

Instead of answering, Tommy spoke to his grandmother. "I—I used the secret key," he whispered conspiratorially. Then he hurried on, indicating the plant she was caressing. "I got it from the windowsill—in your kitchen. It was the reddest one. I—I wanted to bring them all—but they wouldn't fit in the bag. So I just brought this—this reddest one."

He hesitated. "Was that wrong?" he wondered, his voice still low. "Is it still yours? I'll put it back if—"

But she clutched at the plant she held on her lap. Even the helpless hand moved as though to protect it.

"No," she said firmly. "No, that wasn't wrong. Yes. Yes, it's still mine. Thank you for bringing it to me. Thank you, my boy." And she reached forward to lovingly run her hand along the sun-browned cheek.

He looked up at her face in relief. Great relief. He hadn't done wrong. He'd been right. Granny and her geranium were back together. At least a little part of the upside-down world had been righted. He smiled—and she smiled back, and for some reason her smile did not seem quite so crooked as it had been of late.

*S*he hobbled awkwardly to the window so she could watch them go. She didn't have a lace curtain to brush aside. The stiff venetian blinds were always there, though she'd had Tommy's mother lift them so that the red geranium could be placed on the sill to take advantage of the afternoon sun.

Tommy skipped on ahead of his mother, one hand clenched tightly. She knew that he clasped the nickel she had just given him.

A tear trickled down her cheek and moistened her trembling chin. Then she reached up and brushed it away. Her tired back straightened ever so slightly.

She stood until Tommy turned and gave her one more wave, then the van doors slammed shut and the vehicle pulled out of the parking lot. She turned her full attention to the windowsill. She reached out a hand and tenderly snapped the broken leaf stem from the plant before her. One finger probed into the soil of the clay pot.

"I must get some water," she said to herself. "It's a bit dry."

She took one step toward the bathroom taps and was quickly reminded of her cumbersome gait and clumsy hand.

"I must get this useless hand working again," she mused aloud and, her mumbled words seemed to strengthen her resolve. "If I'm going to give proper care to my plant—"

Her murmured thoughts seemed to

hang on the silence of the small room.

Strange, she noticed, turning again to the potted plant in the window— the splash of bright red did make the walls look a bit like rich whipped cream in color.